All net profits from this book will be donated to

charitable organizations, with a gentle preference towards

people with my husband's disease – multiple sclerosis.

Vanita Oelschlager

Acknowledgments

Many Thanks to:

Robin Hegan

Jennie Levy Smith

Kristin Blackwood

Kurt Landefeld

Paul Royer

Cinda Dehner

Mike Blanc

Sheila Tarr

Out of the
BLUE
a book of **color idioms** *and* **silly pictures**

Out of the Blue – Something that happens suddenly and without any warning; totally unexpectedly.

It was a beautiful day when a storm came up *out of the blue*.

This book is dedicated to Gretchen who came to us from out of the blue.
Vanita Oelschlager

Kendall, Kya and Cooper. Mommy loves you!
Robin Hegan

If you feel jealous of what someone
else has, you are green with envy.
When Billy sees my new skateboard,
he will be green with envy.

Green with envy

Show your true colors

If you *show your true colors*, you show what you are really like inside.

When Susie kicked her dog, we saw *her true colors*.

Tickled pink

If something makes you very happy, or pleased, or delighted, you are *tickled pink*.

The Smith twins were *tickled pink* when they got a puppy for Christmas.

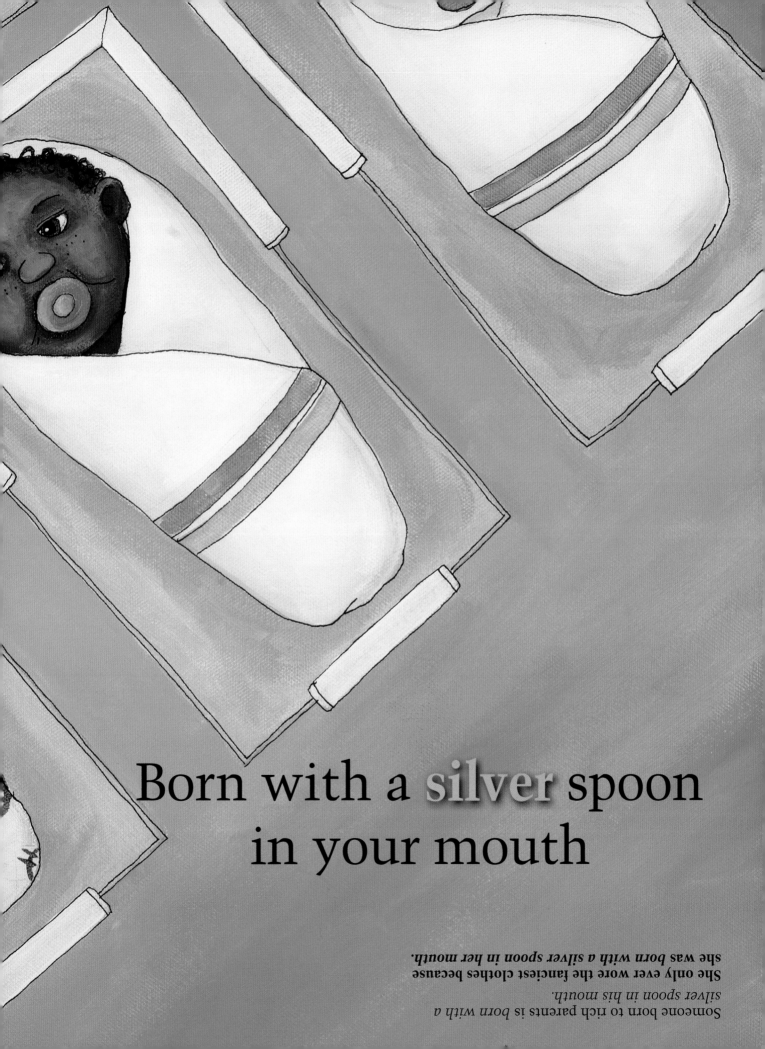

Born with a silver spoon in your mouth

She only ever wore the fanciest clothes because she was born with a silver spoon in her mouth.

Someone born to rich parents is born with a silver spoon in his mouth.

Red-letter day

A day that is very special and makes you happy is a *red-letter day*.

My mom said the day I was born was a *red-letter day* for her.

The *black sheep* in a family or group is the person who is very different or doesn't fit in or is bad. She is the *black sheep* in her family. She is always causing trouble.

Green around the gills

If you feel like you might get sick to your
stomach, you are *green around the gills.*

Riding in a boat in bumpy water, makes
me feel *green around the gills.*

White elephant

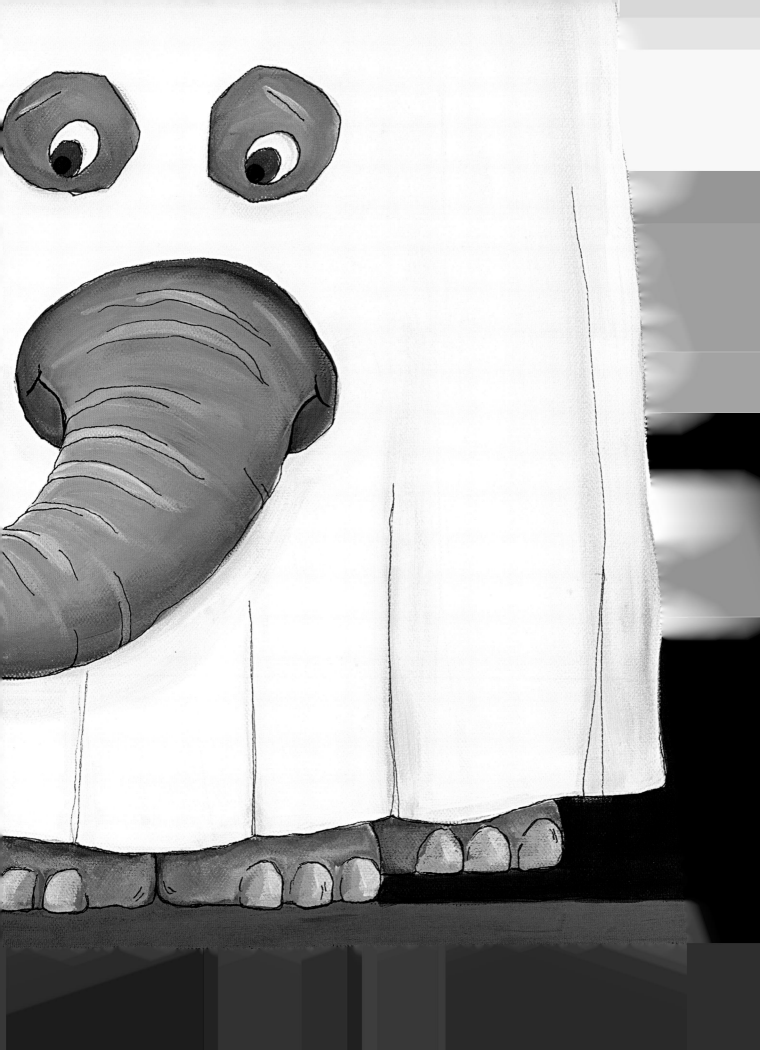

Brown bag it

To take your food in a brown bag when you are going
to be away from home when it is time to eat.
We are all brown bagging it to the park
to spend the day playing.

In the pink

If you are in good health and feeling
well, you are *in the pink*.

**Jim had been sick for weeks,
but now he is *in the pink*.**

Lots of rules and regulations
are called red tape.
We had to go through lots of red tape
to have a parade in the street.

Red tape

A *yellow-bellied* person is a person who is not brave or shows no courage.

I was *yellow-bellied* when I didn't stand up for my brother when people were picking on him.

Yellow-bellied

A *shrinking violet* is a shy person
who doesn't like to talk much and is
uncomfortable with other people.

In her classes, Mary was a
shrinking violet who didn't
raise her hand much.

Shrinking violet

Horse of a different color

A *horse of a different color* is another matter entirely,
or something different than it seemed.
I thought that was her boyfriend, but I found out it
was her brother. That was a horse of a different color.

Once in a blue moon means almost
never, or hardly ever.
Our teacher usually gives us homework, but
once in a blue moon we get the night off.

What are idioms?

Every language has "figures of speech", or idioms. They are kind of a short hand way of explaining something unfamiliar or complicated.

The English language has thousands of them. You cannot understand them because the group of words together has little, often nothing, to do with the meanings of the words taken one by one.

Hundreds of years ago, the words might have meant what they said, but today they do not.

In order to understand a language, you must know what the idioms in that language mean. If you try to figure out the meaning of the idiom word by word you're likely to get nowhere – you will get befuddled or confused. You have to know the "hidden" meaning. You need to read between the lines and behind the words.

I am going to show you the "hidden" meaning of two idioms. Maybe you can find out the "hidden" meaning of some other idioms in this book. Idioms often show a sense of humor. They're your language's ticklish spots so learning them can be lots of fun. I hope you'll enjoy them as much as we do.

Green with envy

Colors often take on other meanings. **Blue** describes sad and lonely feelings. **Red** sometimes means angry. Since about 1600, thanks to William Shakespeare, **green** has been associated with jealousy and desire. He called jealousy "the green sickness" in his play *Antony and Cleopatra*.

Horse of a different color

Whatever the origin of this saying, "horse" stands for an idea and "different color" means a new thought. In the famous movie *The Wizard of Oz* (1939), Dorothy actually rode around in the Emerald City in a buggy pulled by a horse that kept changing colors. She was told that it was "the horse of a different color."

With flying colors

Vanita Oelschlager is a wife, mother, grandmother, former teacher, caregiver, author, and poet. She was named "Writer in Residence" for the Literacy Program at The University of Akron in 2007. She is a graduate of Mount Union College, Alliance, Ohio, where she is currently a member of the Board of Trustees.

Robin Hegan grew up in the Laurel Mountains of Pennsylvania where imagination took her and her childhood friends on many great adventures. After graduating from The Pennsylvania State University with a degree in Integrative Arts, Robin resided in Ohio for several years until she and her husband, Matt, decided to return to the mountains of Pennsylvania to raise their children. Robin's illustrations can also be seen in *My Grampy Can't Walk, Mother Goose Other Goose, Birds of a Feather* and *Life is a Bowl Full of Cherries.* To find out more about Robin, visit www.robinhegan.com.

With Flying Colors – Something happens with ease and great success. One again, the author and the illustrator finished this book with *flying* colors.